The New VP

The New VP

Adapted by Laurie McElroy

Based on "True Jackson, VP Pilot"
episode written by Andy Gordon
Based on "Firing Lulu" written by Dan Kopelman
True Jackson, VP Television Series
created by Andy Gordon

SCHOLASTIC INC.
New York   Toronto   London   Auckland
Sydney   Mexico City   New Delhi   Hong Kong

No part of this work may be reproduced in whole or in part, stored in a retrieval system, or transmitted in any form or by any means, electronic, mechanical, photocopying, recording, or otherwise, without written permission of the publisher. For information regarding permission, write to Scholastic, Inc., Attention: Permissions Department, 557 Broadway, New York, NY 10012.

ISBN: 978-0-545-20028-8

Published by Scholastic Inc.
SCHOLASTIC and associated logos are trademarks and/or registered trademarks of Scholastic Inc.

12 11 10 9 8 7 6 5 4 3 2 1   10 11 12 13 14 15/ 0

Designed by Angela Jun
Printed in the U.S.A.   40
First printing, January 2010

Part 1

True Fashion

Chapter 1

True Jackson squared her shoulders, took a deep breath, and stepped onto the elevator of a New York City skyscraper. She pressed the button for the top floor and didn't exhale until the elevator doors opened again. Then True stepped into the middle of the busy reception area of Mad Style—one of the coolest fashion design companies in the world—and did her best to take in all the sights and sounds. It was a whirlwind.

People rushed around looking important, phones rang, garment racks filled with clothes whizzed by, and a flat-screen monitor on the wall played a Mad Style commercial. True was heading for the receptionist when a guy rushed by with a garment rack full of clothes. Unfortunately, she didn't leap out of the way quite fast enough. True hit the floor with a thud, and then quickly jumped to her feet again.

Did anyone see that? she wondered. The very first thing she did at Mad Style was get trampled by a hit-and-run garment rack. It was totally mortifying, and she was nervous enough already.

True limped over to the receptionist, a man with a headset and a fancy-looking phone setup.

"Hi, I'm not sure where I'm supposed to go," True told him with a nervous smile.

"Are you visiting your mommy?" the receptionist asked. His tone was a little sarcastic.

True smiled again. "No, I'm True Jackson," she answered. "The new vice president."

The receptionist—True later learned that his name was Oscar—suddenly changed his attitude, and his tone of voice. "You're right in there," he said, pointing to an office across the floor.

"Thanks," True said, heading in that direction. She stopped and turned back to Oscar. "Oh, and I like your scarf," she said.

"Oh," Oscar put his hand on his scarf and beamed at her. Usually vice presidents breezed past him as if he wasn't even there. True had actually taken the time to notice him and pay him a compliment. He was touched.

True knew what he was thinking—what everyone at Mad

Style was thinking. How did a fifteen-year-old high school girl get to be vice president of anything, let alone a multimillion dollar fashion company?

It all started the Friday before. True was trying to earn extra money for the summer by selling lunches at Manhattan office buildings. She chose her favorite area in the whole city — the Garment District — and set herself up in the lobby of the Mad Style building with a big cooler and a handmade sign that read: True's Sandwiches.

Ever since True could remember, she had two wishes. The first was for world peace. The second would be to have her own fashion line. She absolutely loved designing and making clothes. She started making clothes for her dolls when she was little, but now she made things for herself. It was her passion.

Right then, just being near the fashion industry was exciting enough for her. She exchanged sandwiches for dollars. Her friend Ryan, who held a basket with a YOU CHIPPIN? sign, handed out bags of chips and pretzels.

True remembered giving someone a ham-and-cheese sandwich, and taking their money with a smile and a thank you. She was turning out to be a pretty good salesperson, she thought.

Ryan was laid-back and totally confident when it came to pretty much everything he did, but he still had some things to learn about sales. "All sales are final," he said, handing a woman a bag of chips. "So we apologize if the sandwiches cause you to throw up or get the poopies."

Was he trying to destroy her business before she even got started? "Ryan!" True yelled, watching her customers walk away.

"What?" Ryan asked. "It's called being polite."

True took the basket from him. "Why don't you go see if it's raining," she said.

"It's not raining," Ryan told her. He knew when someone was trying to get rid of him, and that's exactly what True was doing.

"How do you know? Did you check?" True asked.

Suddenly Ryan wasn't so sure. He hadn't checked. He couldn't say with absolute certainty that it wasn't raining. "No," he said, trudging off to check the sky.

True sighed with relief and watched him walk away. She hoped that he would get interested in something else for a little while—at least until the lunch rush was over. Having Ryan nearby was great fun when things were slow, but he was definitely bad for business.

A man was walking toward her flipping through the pages of a portfolio and checking his email on his fancy cell phone at the same time. True gasped. She recognized him from his

pictures in all the fashion magazines. He was fashion icon Max Madigan—the head of Mad Style. He was one of True's idols.

A woman dressed in black trailed behind him. True recognized her, too—Amanda Cantwell, one of Mad Style's top designers.

True got goose bumps just being this close to the two of them.

"I don't care if they loved it in Milan," Mr. Madigan said to Amanda. "We're not making solid-gold bathing suits. It's not functional."

Amanda trotted behind him on very high heels. "Functional, no. Fabulous, yes!" she said, throwing her arms out dramatically.

True saw her opportunity. Maybe—if she sold sandwiches to them every day—important people like Mr. Madigan and Amanda Cantwell would teach her about the fashion industry. Maybe they'd even look at her designs. Plus, these were exactly the kind of customers she needed—people too busy and too important to go out and get lunch.

"Would you like a sandwich?" she asked with a big grin. "They say lunch is the second most important meal of the day. Third if you count dinner."

Mr. Madigan was won over by her enthusiasm. "Well, I am a bit peckish," he said, patting his stomach.

"Then you're in luck." True grabbed a sandwich from her cooler. "Today's special is ham and Swiss on homemade potato bread. I hope you like smiling," she told him.

"I do. I do like smiling," Mr. Madigan answered. He handed True a bill. "Here you go," he said.

"Thanks," she said, exchanging his money for a sandwich.

Mr. Madigan started to walk toward the elevator, and then turned back to True. "Young woman, may I ask who made your jacket?"

"Well, you did," True said.

"I thought it looked familiar," Mr. Madigan said. "But I don't recall the buttons being orange."

"They weren't," True said, looking down at her buttons. "I changed them." That was another thing True had been doing since she was a little girl, making changes to the clothes she bought to make them more fun, more fashionable, and more True. But she was a little embarrassed to be telling Mr. Madigan that she had changed his design.

Mr. Madigan didn't seem to mind at all. In fact, he liked it! "Good! Perfect!" he said. "Why?"

"Well, originally they were blue, but the blue was just sort of—" True tried to come up with a nice way to tell him that blue was so last year. She couldn't. "—ugh," she said finally. "But the orange makes it fun!" she added brightly.

The elevator doors opened with a *ping*.

"Max. Elevator," Amanda said.

But Mr. Madigan was more interested in True and her changes to his designs. "And the pants?" he asked.

"They're yours, too, sort of," True said, looking down at her cropped pants. She remembered that they were full-length when she bought them. But they looked better cropped, especially with her short jacket. "I shortened them."

Amanda was still holding the elevator doors open, and the other people on board were beginning to grumble. "Max," she said.

Mr. Madigan smiled at True and joined his colleague on the elevator. "Amanda, who's the youngest person we have on staff?" he asked.

"That would be me," Amanda told him happily.

"Huh," he answered.

Amanda's smile started to fade.

"Why don't we have anyone really young?" he asked, pointing at True. "Like that girl."

"Why doesn't a hundred million dollar fashion empire employ children?" she asked. "Gee," she scoffed, "that's a tough one."

The elevator doors were closing. Mr. Madigan put his hand out to stop them. He handed his sandwich to Amanda and stepped back into the lobby. "Young lady," he said.

"What are you doing?" Amanda asked, following him.

Mr. Madigan ignored her. He zeroed in on True. "How would you like to be the newest vice president of Mad Style?"

Amanda gasped.

True laughed. "Quit playing," she said.

"I'm not playing," Mr. Madigan said seriously. "I want you to be my VP of youth apparel."

True didn't quite know what to say. She had hoped to rub elbows with the fashion bigwigs this summer, but a job at Mad Style was beyond her wildest dreams. She didn't even know if she could say yes without permission. "Well, I'll have to ask my mom, but that sounds great!"

"Great. We're on the top floor," Mr. Madigan told her. "You start Monday." He got on the elevator and started texting instructions to the human resources department. True would need an office.

Amanda followed him with a frown.

"See what I did there?" Mr. Madigan asked her with a confident laugh.

All Amanda could do was glare at him. The last thing she wanted in the office was a little kid—a high school girl who liked to change perfectly fabulous Amanda Cantwell fashions—competing with her to be top designer.

That had all happened on Friday, and now it was Monday morning and she was walking into her very own office at Mad Style. True still had to pinch herself every once in a while to make sure she wasn't dreaming. She was totally excited to be there. There was just one problem. She had no idea what a vice president for youth apparel was supposed to do.

Chapter 2

True's office was huge! She had an amazing view of the city. There was a desk, a drawing table, a couch, and a shiny black chair. She sat in it, and slipped right off and onto the floor with a very loud thud! She had only been at Mad Style for five minutes and already she had fallen twice.

She heard someone come into the office. "I'm okay," she said, mortified to be seen on the floor again.

"Is the rug to your liking?" a woman asked in a sarcastic tone of voice.

"Hi. Sorry." True jumped to her feet. "I'm supposed to be here," she said, extending her hand. "I'm True and . . ."

The woman shook True's hand with an unhappy expression. "I was expecting you," she said. "I'm Cricket, your" — she had to swallow her distaste before she could get the word out—"assistant."

True's jaw dropped. "My assistant? For real?"

Cricket responded with a sullen nod.

"I've never had an assistant before," True said happily.

"You don't say," Cricket answered.

True was too surprised to pay attention to Cricket's tone of voice. "Although, my school did have an auction once and I got the math teacher to be my butler for a day." True laughed, remembering how much fun it was to order a teacher around. "I was all, 'More pancakes, Mr. Jameson.'" She laughed even harder. Being her teacher's boss was a total hoot.

Cricket simply stared and waited for True to stop laughing. She didn't even crack a smile. "Anyway, my desk is out there," she said, pointing to the reception area. "Let me know if you need anything."

"Like what?" True asked.

"I don't know. Research. Schedules. Something to drink," Cricket answered.

"Well, I am kind of thirsty," True said. "If you could point me towards the water fountain, I'll go—"

Cricket cut her off. "There's a refrigerator built behind this wall." She picked up a remote and pressed a button. One of the walls in True's office opened up. Behind it were a small

refrigerator, a microwave oven, a flat screen TV, a coffee maker, and all kinds of fun gadgets. There was even a supply of microwave popcorn!

True's eyes widened. "Oh my gosh!" she yelled, running over to the wall. "This is so fun!" She opened the refrigerator. It was stocked with soft drinks. "I'm not supposed to drink soda," she told Cricket. "It makes my tongue sweat." She checked the refrigerator again. "Is there any bubbly water?"

"I can order you some," Cricket said, making a note. "Would you like some juice boxes while I'm at it?" she drawled.

True totally missed Cricket's mocking tone. "For real?" she asked excitedly. Then she noticed the expression on her assistant's face. "Or are you just being snotty?" she asked.

Cricket rolled her eyes. "Snotty," she admitted. "But I can have your refrigerator stocked however you like."

"Cool," True said with a nod. "Oh, do you think it would be okay to bring in some chairs from home? That one's kind of slippy," she said, pointing to the shiny black chair that had dumped her on the floor a few minutes ago.

"There are furniture catalogs on your desk," Cricket said. "Circle whatever you want."

True's surly assistant was on her way back to her own desk when True's best friend Lulu raced into the office, almost

knocking Cricket down. She hugged True with an excited scream.

True screamed, too. She was starting to feel like a total alien at Mad Style, and she was relieved and excited to see a friendly face. Lulu was always a huge ball of energy, and True couldn't ask for a better, more loyal friend.

"That's my best friend. We met in space camp," Lulu said to Cricket. "Oh, little heads up. You don't even get to go to space," she said. "It's kind of a rip." Then True remembered that she hadn't introduced her friend and her assistant yet.

"Oh, Lulu," she said, waving her over. "This is Cricket, my assistant."

Lulu was ready to say hello, but the word *assistant* threw her for a loop. "Seriously? You're her boss?" she asked True.

True nodded and Lulu turned to Cricket. "But you're so old!" she exclaimed.

Cricket stiffened.

"Lulu!" True yelled. She loved her best friend, but Lulu had a bad habit of saying whatever was on her mind without thinking things through first. Like now. She didn't stop to think that calling Cricket old might be kind of insulting.

"But you're a kid," Lulu said to True, defending herself. "And she's a grown woman. It's like

14

backwards day." Lulu skipped across the room to check out the view.

"I'm sorry, Cricket," True said.

Cricket rolled her eyes. "Not as sorry as I am," she said, heading for her desk.

Lulu leaned against True's desk. "Wait. This is your office?" she asked.

True laughed. "Check it out! I've got a view of Fifth Avenue, and you see this wall over here?"

"Um hmm," Lulu murmured.

"You see it?" True asked again. She made sure Lulu was watching when she picked up the remote and pressed the button. The wall opened. "It turns into a refrigerator," True said.

Lulu gasped. "Not even!"

True put the remote down. "And I get to decorate this office any way I want. They even gave me catalogs."

Lulu was still stuck on the amazing, magical wall. She grabbed the remote and made the wall close, then open. Close, then open. Close, then open. She couldn't stop!

The noise was starting to get to True. Plus she could see that people in the reception area were watching. Watching and laughing.

"Stop it," True said.

Lulu kept opening and closing the wall.

"Lulu!" True yelled. "Lulu!"

Lulu didn't hear. She was totally mesmerized.

True really yelled now. "Dude!"

Lulu finally heard her. "Sorry," she said, putting down the remote. "Okay. Sorry," she said again, throwing herself over the back of the couch and plopping her feet on top of the coffee table.

Amanda Cantwell trotted in on her stilettos carrying a fruit basket. "Oh good, you're all set up," she said, dropping the basket onto Lulu's lap as if she wasn't even there. "Welcome!" she said. "Everything okay so far?" she asked with fake enthusiasm.

True hoped Amanda would turn out to be a really supportive teacher. She knew she had a lot to learn. "Yeah, I was just about to come and—"

"Great, if you have any questions about the job, my door is always open," Amanda said, loud enough for the whole office to hear.

True was so relieved. If Amanda was willing to answer questions, learning her new job would be so much easier. "Really?" she asked.

Amanda lowered her voice and shook her head. "No."

True sighed. She was afraid of that. Amanda hadn't exactly been thrilled when Mr. Madigan hired her.

Lulu, meanwhile, was going through the fruit basket looking for something good to eat—like candy or a brownie. All she found were apples. "Nope," she said, throwing a Granny Smith apple on the floor. She picked up a Red Delicious and chucked that to the floor as well. "No," she said, grabbing another green apple. "Not doing that!"

She stopped when she realized True and Amanda were watching her.

"Enjoying that, are we?" Amanda snapped.

"Not really, it's, like, ninety percent apples," Lulu told her.

True made a cutting motion across her neck and motioned Lulu to eat. She was going to have to win Amanda over. Lulu trashing the gift Amanda had brought her was going to make that harder.

Lulu held an apple up to her mouth. "I like apples," she mumbled, pretending to take a bite.

"Well, anyway," Amanda said, turning back to True. "I'm sure you're anxious to get busy." She started to rush out of the office.

"Actually, I do have a question," True said.

Amanda stopped and put her hands on her hips. "Go."

"What am I supposed to be doing?" True asked.

"Well, you should be playing jacks in a schoolyard somewhere," Amanda snapped. "But since you're here, let me run it down for you."

Amanda picked up the latest Mad Style design book and flipped through the pages as she talked. "Mad Style makes and distributes a wide variety of fashion lines. High-end couture, working women, daily wear, and yes"—she shot a look at True—"youth apparel.

"That's where you come in," Amanda said brightly. "Overseeing the designs for little boys and girls."

"Wait," True said. "So I get to think up the designs?"

"Yes, 'thinking' is one of your responsibilities," Amanda mocked, putting air quotes around the word.

True rolled her eyes. She was getting more than a little tired of all the sarcasm. All she did was ask a question. People at Mad Style were so mean!

Amanda kept talking, reeling off a list of things True had to do. With each item, she sped her speech up a little more. By the end she was talking so fast that True's ears could hardly keep up.

"There's also approval, testing, marketing, and production," she said. "There's a lot that can go wrong, and not enough time to get it done, so your eyes have to be on the ball

at all times." Amanda pointed to her own eyes and then at a series of imaginary balls she was juggling in the air. "Miss a deadline," Amanda said, snapping her fingers dramatically. "The whole machine falls apart. Do you understand?"

True felt like those invisible balls Amanda was juggling had all just landed in the pit of her stomach—and they were heavy. "No," she said.

"Good!" Amanda said happily. She swept out of the room, saying loudly enough for the entire floor to hear, "My door is always open."

True watched her go. *Yeah, right*, she thought. *Open and ready to slam in my face—except when people are listening.*

Lulu watched her go and then turned to True and made a pinched-up face.

"I know, right?" True said. She shook off her heavy feeling. Mr. Madigan had hired her for reason. She had great fashion sense. But first, she needed to apply some of that fashion sense to her office. She couldn't very well do her best work in a space that didn't feel like hers, could she? Her first order of business was decorating her new office. "Let's go check out these catalogs," she said to Lulu.

Lulu followed True over to her desk. "So, you can order anything you want?" Lulu asked, hopping onto the top of the desk.

"That's what they said," True told her, flipping through a catalog. She handed another one to Lulu. "Look for big couches. I want comfortable furniture."

Lulu gasped. "The Pinks are totally going to freak when they hear you have a job in an office." Then she thought about it for a second. "I hope it doesn't make them mad."

The Pinks were a group of popular girls who went to True and Lulu's high school. They liked to be the first at everything. Nothing made them madder than being overshadowed in the cool department.

True rolled her eyes. She'd rather be happy than popular, and The Pinks didn't seem very happy to her. They were always cutting other people down. "Why do you care what they think?" she asked. "They're just a bunch of good-looking bullies in matching outfits."

"I can't help it; they're just so popular," Lulu said defensively. "I'm incapable of resistance." Then she spotted something that completely changed the conversation. "Oh, look! A disco ball." She flung her arms out like a disco queen doing the hustle.

"Lulu, this is an office," True explained. "I need furniture that's going to make me look professional. You know, like I know what I'm doing."

"All right," Lulu said quietly, trying to be serious and professional.

20

Then True spotted something really fun and exciting. "Oh! An indoor trampoline!"

The girls were laughing over the picture when Cricket opened the door and poked her head into True's office.

"I'm sorry to interrupt, but they want you to sit in on the business-wear meeting," Cricket said.

"I thought I was only doing the kid's clothes," True said. What did she know about business wear?

Cricket shrugged. "I don't know. They just said it was very, very, very important that you're in the meeting by ten."

"Well, what time is it now?" True asked.

Cricket suppressed a smile. "Ten-fifteen," she said.

"Oh, no," True moaned. Late for her first meeting! She raced out of her office and into the reception area. She ran right into a guy carrying an armload of papers. He went flying and so did they. They fluttered all over the place. "Sorry!" True said, wincing. She wanted to help the guy pick everything up, but she was already fifteen minutes behind schedule. If this was school, she'd get detention.

True suddenly realized she didn't even know where to go. She spotted Oscar. At least he was nice. "Conference room?" she asked.

He pointed down the hall. The guy she knocked over was grumbling and gathering his papers. True hurdled over his head and raced in the direction Oscar had pointed. With any luck, she wouldn't get fired on her very first morning.

Chapter 3

True stopped short when she got to a room that looked like it was the conference room. Amanda paced in the doorway checking her watch. A lot of people True hadn't met yet were seated at two long tables facing each other. In between them was a raised runway, like the ones in fashion shows.

"Sorry I'm late," True said. "But I was in my office and I just heard—"

Amanda shushed her. "There's no excuse for lateness," she said, pointing to a seat. She sounded just like a mean teacher.

"Right," True said.

She took her seat just as Mr. Madigan rushed in. "Sorry I'm late," he said breezily. He was busy texting someone on his cell phone and barely looked up.

Amanda's reaction to her boss's lateness was totally different than her reaction to True's. "Oh, are you?" she said with a giggle. "I hadn't even noticed." She laughed again. "We haven't even started yet."

Mr. Madigan walked right past Amanda and over to True. "Hi, True. How's it going so far?"

"Great," True said. "There's a refrigerator! In my office!"

"I've got one, too," Mr. Madigan said. "Isn't it cool?"

"Yes!" True told him.

Amanda cleared her throat to get their attention. "Shall we?" she asked.

Mr. Madigan nodded and took the seat next to True's while Amanda ran to the end of the runway. She stopped to put on a headset so that her words would be amplified, and clapped her hands for attention. Classical music began to play, and the curtain behind her opened.

Amanda marched down the runway. "Behold! The fall line of the modern person's business collection."

She stepped aside and a model strutted down the runway wearing a black dress. A man in a black suit and a dark gray tie was just behind her, followed by a woman in another black suit.

"Last year, gray was the new black," Amanda told the room. "Well, this year, black is the new black! It's *baaaaaaaack* to black!"

24

The models stood at the end of the runway so that everyone could get a good look at their clothes.

Mr. Madigan got up and walked over to them, checking out the details on the outfits. "Nice lines," he said thoughtfully. "Strong silhouette. Good detailing." He considered the clothes for a few more moments. "True, what do you think?" he asked.

"Me?" True asked. She was totally panicked. It was her first meeting and she had no idea what to say. "I don't know," she said slowly, getting to her feet. Then she remembered that Mr. Madigan had hired her because he liked her opinions, and she had one now. There was way too much black on that runway. People were going to work, not to a funeral.

"What if the cuffs were yellow?" she asked.

Amanda cringed. "Yellow?" she shouted.

Mr. Madigan shot her a look. He liked his employees to be free to share their opinions. They couldn't do that if they were afraid of being shouted at.

"I mean, yellow?" Amanda asked in a much quieter, kinder tone of voice.

True swallowed. "Just a hint, maybe," she said. "I mean, it just feels like it needs some color."

Amanda bit her thumb. "I know you've been in this business since breakfast," she said. "But with all due respect, yellow

25

cuffs are the worst idea since reversible sweaters." She laughed dismissively.

"Are you tripping?" True asked. "I like reversible sweaters. I have a holiday one with a turkey on one side and a snowman on the other. It's too cute."

Amanda pushed one of the models out of her way. "Well, we all have things that make us happy. Mine is working with adults," she snapped. She turned to Mr. Madigan. "Max."

She didn't get the support she wanted. Amanda couldn't believe it, but Mr. Madigan seemed to be taking True's suggestion seriously. He was actually considering changing Amanda's designs because a high school girl told him to!

Mr. Madigan walked over to True. "Stop tripping, Amanda," he said. "I understand what she's saying. These designs are good, but are they too safe?" he asked.

Amanda raised her hand to answer the question. "Oh, I'll take this one," she said. "No."

But Mr. Madigan's wheels were already turning. He picked up a piece of red fabric and studied the black women's suit. "A hint of color might be daring," he said, walking over to the model and holding the fabric next to her jacket. "Like a jazzy pattern inside." He turned to True for her reaction.

"Or a pink feather on the shoulder," she said.

"Or a single blue button, and then a red one," Mr. Madigan said.

Amanda put her hands on her hips, totally outraged. Her boss and his new vice president were redesigning her clothes without any input at all from her. And they were perfect to begin with.

True and Mr. Madigan didn't notice. They were busy trading ideas and getting more and more excited about the possibilities.

"I like that!" True said, pointing at him.

"Me, too," Mr. Madigan touched his finger against True's and made a sizzling sound.

Amanda clapped her hands. "People! People!" she shouted. "Is there a gas leak in the building?"

Mr. Madigan turned to her.

"Pink feathers?" Amanda asked, practically spitting out the words. "Yellow cuffs?" she snapped, glaring at True. "We make clothes for working men and women. Not clowns and leprechauns."

True knew that wasn't fair. She might be young. She might be new to the fashion business. But if there was one thing she knew about, it was clothes. And all black was all boring. People needed color to brighten up their lives. That wasn't clownish.

That was cool. "Just because it's work doesn't mean it can't be fun," she said.

"I can see it now," Mr. Madigan said, walking across the room. He was clearly excited about this new idea. "Slogan—Put Some Color in Your Week!" He thought about that for a second. "Yes! Wow!" He clapped his hands together.

"You've got a lot of work to do," he said to True and Amanda. "A lot of work." He held the red fabric over his eyes. "And if it's not all done by noon tomorrow, I'm going to fire . . ."

Amanda knew what was coming. She ducked just in time.

Mr. Madigan waved his arm back and forth, and then landed on one person. "That guy," he said.

The guy swallowed nervously. He shot a look at True and then studied his notes. Clearly, he didn't think she would make her deadline. That meant he would be hitting the unemployment line. True wasn't sure whether Mr. Madigan was joking or serious. He was so nice, he had to be joking. Right?

"Don't let me down," Mr. Madigan said. He threw the red fabric on the table and walked out of the room.

True turned to Amanda for a clue as to what had just happened. But all Amanda did was cross her arms and look away. Mr. Madigan was right when he said there was a lot of work to do, and True was obviously on her own.

When True got back to her office, she found Ryan sitting on the shiny black chair reading a magazine.

"Hey, Ryan, what are you doing here?" she asked.

"Oh, just reading this awesome article," he said, closing the magazine. He read the headline on the front cover. "Designers pick their favorite textures. It's really . . ." He let his head fall forward and pretended to snore.

True laughed. She loved reading that article, but fashion was definitely not Ryan's thing. Then she noticed that he was sitting in the shiny black chair — the one that had thrown her to the floor that morning. "Wait a minute, how are you sitting in that chair?" she asked.

"Duct tape," Ryan said simply.

True heard the sound of the tape ripping as Ryan got to his feet. The back of his shirt and the chair were both covered in silver tape. True laughed. *Leave it to Ryan to find a way to sit in an un-sittable chair*, she thought.

Lulu wandered into the office. "So they're swapping out your couch for a cooler one. I talked to Charlotte," she said.

"Who is Charlotte?" True asked.

Lulu pointed toward the reception area with a confused

expression. "She works down the hall with Josie and Quincy," she said.

How was it that Lulu knew all these people already and True knew no one?

"It's not a block party, Lulu. I work here," True said.

"Hey, I wish I worked here," Ryan said. He threw his arms out. "This place is ri*donk*ulous!" He sat on True's desk. "So, how's it going?"

"Oh, great!" True said sarcastically. "Everyone hates me."

Ryan found that hard to believe. "Oh c'mon, who would hate you?" he asked.

"Ha! Everyone," Lulu said with a laugh. "Ella in accounting called her a junior execu-turd!"

True rolled her eyes. While she was in the meeting, Lulu must have met everyone in the entire office — and all of them were making fun of True!

Ryan changed the subject. "All right, check this out. I got you a new screen saver."

"How did you get on my computer?" True asked.

"Well, I don't want to get too technical, but I banged on the side until it turned on," Ryan joked. He sat behind True's desk and turned the monitor around so that she could see it. He had replaced the very professional Mad Style wallpaper with a big picture of himself in front of a blue sky with white puffy clouds.

Ryan clicked the keyboard, and the picture of his head screamed and then it split open. A picture of an oozing, bloody brain replaced it, and then that split in half and disappeared, too. The blue sky in the background turned into a field of fire. A monsterlike voice intoned, "Ryan Rules," as the letters appeared on the screen. They were drippy and blood-colored.

True stared at her friend, speechless. Did he really expect her to keep that as her screen saver at work?

"That's right," Ryan said proudly.

True headed back to the couch. She was about to ask him to change it back when Amanda stormed into her office, practically hidden under a pile of black clothing.

"Yellow cuffs," Amanda yelled. "Yellow cuffs," she said again, dropping the clothes on top of True. "Do you know how long it took me to write the line 'Black is back'?"

Lulu and Ryan didn't realize the question was a sarcastic one. They thought it was real, and started guessing.

"I've got this one. Five seconds," Ryan said.

"I'm going to say twenty," Lulu said. "No ten!"

Ryan agreed. "Ten seconds. That's our final answer!" he said, pounding his hand on the desk.

Amanda glared. "Who are you children?" she asked.

Ryan pretended to be amused. "Children?" he asked with a chuckle. "Look, lady, I don't know what country you're from, but here in America we don't let children carry guns." He walked around the front of True's desk and raised his arms like a weight lifter to show off what he lovingly called his guns—his biceps. "Bam!" he shouted, flexing his muscles.

Amanda screamed and jumped back.

"Oh, yeah." Ryan flashed her a grin and kissed the muscle on his right arm. "They frighten me, too."

Amanda turned her attention back to True. "News flash. You're on your own for this one," she said. "You want color in the outfits? Fine!" She dropped another dress on True's lap. "You redesign them," she said, leaning on the back of the couch. "You better make a fresh pot of coffee," she sneered.

True stared at her, dismayed. "I'm not even allowed to drink coffee," she said.

"Well, then eat a fistful of jellybeans," Amanda snapped. "There's work to be done."

Ryan watched Amanda storm out of the office. "Wow, she seems really nice," he joked.

Lulu laughed, but True was serious—seriously scared.

"What am I going to do?" she asked her friends. "I can't do all this by myself."

"Well, you're not by yourself. You've go the A-Team with you," Ryan said. He threw his arm around Lulu and they both smiled at their friend.

"Really? You'd stay and help me?" True asked.

"Sure," Ryan said with a shrug. "I mean, I was going to play video games, but making dresses sounds fun." Suddenly he realized what he had just said, and how un-manly that sounded. *He was spending way too much time with girls,* he thought. "Did you hear what I just said?" he asked. "I've got to go."

He started to leave the office, but Lulu knew her friend needed help—as much help as she could get. She threw herself onto Ryan's back and tackled him to the floor.

Ryan was going to help them make dresses, whether he wanted to or not. But right now he was totally confused. "Did I get the first down, Coach?" he asked limply.

Chapter 4

By the next morning, True's drawing table had become their base of operations. The supplies they needed were all within reach. True stood in the middle of her two friends, and, like a surgeon, asked for the instruments she needed to save those suits from a life of dull, boring black.

"Thread," she said, holding out her left hand to Lulu.

Lulu placed a spool of pink thread into True's hand. "Thread."

"Scissors," True said, holding her right hand out to Ryan.

Ryan gave her what she needed. "Scissors."

True snipped a thread. The tools weren't enough. She needed more. "Pep talk," she said.

"You're doing great," Lulu told her.

"Thank you." True bent over her "patient" and made a final adjustment. "One final cut," she said. "There; I've done all I can," she said looking at Ryan. "Would you like to close?" she joked.

Ryan acted like an intern about to operate on his first patient. "Of course," he said seriously.

Lulu spotted a guy walking past True's office. He was young. And he was cute! "Whoa, who was that?" she asked.

"Who?" True said.

Lulu grabbed True's arm and pulled her out into doorway. "Him!" she squealed.

True watched the guy walk across the floor. She noticed that he was carrying drumsticks. "I've never seen him before," True said.

Lulu gaped at him. He was seriously cute. "Maybe he's a model."

"I don't think so," True said.

"Not messy enough?" Lulu asked.

"That, and he's pushing a mail cart," True said.

Lulu grabbed True's arm again and pulled her into the reception area so that they could follow the cute guy around. "C'mon."

"Cut it out, Lulu. This is a place of business," True told her.

"He can't see us," Lulu pointed out. The guy had his back to them.

"Nope," the guy said. "But I can hear you."

Lulu ducked behind a tall plant. True was left standing out in the open. She gave the guy an embarrassed smile and noticed that his eyes were very, very blue.

Once again, Lulu grabbed True's arm and pulled her behind the plant. Then she held the plant in front of the two of them while they tiptoed back to True's office.

"That was embarrassing," True said when they were finally safe in the privacy of her own office.

"Yeah. Why'd you make me do that?" Lulu asked.

True shot her a look, and then noticed that her drawing table was empty.

"Where are the suits?" she asked Ryan.

Ryan was busy on her computer. He didn't look up. "I threw them on the couch," he said.

True's jaw dropped. The couch was gone. "Where is the couch?" she yelled.

"The couch guys came for it," Ryan said, still not looking up. Suddenly, he realized what had happened. He had just sat there while the couch guys left with the suits. All of True's hard work — gone!

True and Lulu stared at him, shocked and angry.

Panic was starting to form in the pit of True's stomach.

Ryan jumped to his feet. "Look, everything's going to be fine," he said. "I'm going to get them and we'll be happy again." He raced across True's office and into the reception area. He banged into the very same guy True had rammed into the day before. Once again, his papers flew all over the office.

Ryan raised his hands up in the air. "I don't work here," he said and kept walking. He stopped at Oscar's desk in the middle of the reception area. "Hey, did you see some guys come through here with a couch?" he asked.

"Yes," Oscar told him.

"Okay, there were suits on the couch. Did they take those, too," Ryan asked desperately.

"No," Oscar said.

Ryan breathed a big sigh of relief. "Oh, thank goodness."

"They threw them down the trash shoot," Oscar told him.

The trash shoot? Ryan blanched. "Oh come on," he yelled.

He raced across the floor. True and Lulu were right behind him. If they were going to save True's job — and that random guy's, too — they were going to have to find those suits. If that meant following the trash shoot to the basement then that was what they would have to do. Garbage or no garbage.

True, Lulu, and Ryan were knee-high in garbage, searching for the suits. The room in the sub-basement where the building's garbage was collected was dark and smelly and disgusting. True thought she might have seen something moving in the corner. She didn't want to look too closely.

True dumped a trash bag out on the floor. "My gosh. This is the nastiest place I've ever been in my entire—" She was about to say "life" when she turned and spotted Ryan—chewing! "Ryan, what are you eating?" she shouted.

Ryan looked up with a guilty expression. "Well, it's either a ham sandwich or the handle to an old briefcase," he admitted. "Either way, I'm not sharing." He quickly shoved the rest of the mystery item into his mouth.

True shuddered at the idea of sharing whatever it was, and then looked around the trash room again. She felt totally defeated. "Okay, this is hopeless," she said. "We've been down here for a half an hour. We're never going to find those suits."

"It'll be all right," Lulu said.

"Yeah, True," Ryan agreed. "I mean, if there's anything I've learned from you, it's that things are never as bad as they seem, so—" Suddenly an enormous amount of trash came down the shoot and fell directly on Ryan's head.

Lulu laughed.

True could only shake her head. Being hit in the head with garbage seemed exactly right after everything else that had happened since she arrived at Mad Style. "You know what? Maybe this is a sign. Maybe I'm in over my head," she said. "This was supposed to be the best summer ever, but now here I am, searching though garbage, trying to save a job I'm not even sure I can do."

Lulu and Ryan listened seriously. True was always so upbeat. So positive. If she felt defeated then things were bad — really bad.

True let out a big sigh. "I think I have to quit," she said, heading for the door.

Lulu stopped her. "True, this is everything you've always wanted."

"I know," True said sadly. She didn't add the words "and I failed," but that's how she felt. She took one last look at the trash room and left.

Ryan shook his head. "This is all my fault. I feel terrible. I feel like—"

Suddenly another big pile of garbage fell from the trash chute and onto his head.

"Oh come on, man!" Ryan yelled. Was his day not bad enough already? He had destroyed his best friend's chance at the career of her dreams. Did the universe really have to throw garbage at him, too?

True got off the elevator on the top floor, ready to go see Mr. Madigan and tell him she wasn't up to doing the job he had hired her to do. He was nice. But everyone else at Mad Style was making everything too hard. When so many people wanted her to fail, how could she win?

On the way to his office she walked past Cricket and Amanda having coffee with another woman. They didn't see True.

"You know, she has a bunch of children helping her," Cricket said.

"Ugh, that's terrible," Amanda said with a shudder. "Children shouldn't be making clothes. Unless it's in a factory somewhere."

All the women laughed at Amanda's joke, but True was shocked. She had learned about children being exploited in factories in third world countries, and it was nothing to laugh about. She couldn't believe Amanda would even make a joke like that.

"Do you think she'll make the deadline?" Amanda asked Cricket.

True's assistant shrugged. "Who knows? She seems to have the attention span of a rabbit."

"Well, I know one thing. She is not sitting at our table during lunch," Amanda said.

True trudged toward Oscar. It was bad enough that she had failed at her job, but she was also surrounded by a bunch of mean girls. Weren't grown-ups supposed to act better than that?

True fought back tears, but Oscar saw everything. He handed True a tissue as she passed by. She wiped her eyes and blew her nose on the way to Mr. Madigan's office. It was time to quit.

She knocked on the door, ready to confess to Mr. Madigan that she had let him down.

"Come in."

True started speaking before she could lose her nerve. "Mr. Madigan, I'm sorry, but I—" She stopped short when she realized that she wasn't talking to Mr. Madigan. The cute guy from the mailroom—Lulu had learned his name was Jimmy—was sitting behind Mr. Madigan's desk, drumming on water bottles.

"Hey, what are you doing in here?" True asked.

Jimmy twirled a drumstick between his fingers. "Rocking out."

41

"Aren't you going to get in trouble being in Mr. Madigan's office?" she said.

"Nah. You call him Mr. Madigan. I call him Uncle Max," Jimmy told her.

"Oh," True said quietly. Suddenly she was embarrassed and didn't know what to say.

"You know, you look pretty good when you don't have a plant on your head," Jimmy joked.

Now True was even more embarrassed. "Well, you know, that was just my best friend Lulu, you know, girlfriend and girlfriend, one girlfriend be acting crazy, you know how it goes, you know . . ." True realized she was babbling. "It wasn't me."

"Okay, calm down. It's cool," Jimmy said. "So, are you having fun?"

"Here?" True asked. She was shocked that anyone would even ask that question. Hadn't he heard what people were saying about her?

"Yeah," he answered.

True had thought working at Mad Style was going to be fun and exciting, but now that she had spent a couple of hours in the office her answer was totally different. "No."

"Oh." Jimmy gave her a sympathetic look. "What's the problem?" he asked.

Suddenly, True realized that the problem wasn't just that she was going to miss her deadline. The bigger problem was that most of the people in the office *wanted* her to miss the deadline. Especially Amanda. In fact, if Amanda had helped True the way she was supposed to, none of this would have happened. But she couldn't say all that to Jimmy. "I don't know," she answered. "It's hard. Some of the people are sort of mean."

"Yeah. It can be pretty high school here sometimes," Jimmy said.

Something started to click in True's brain. "What'd you say?" she asked.

"Working here. It's like high school," the drummer told her. "The cliques, the egos, the homework."

"I hadn't thought of it like that," True said thoughtfully. Suddenly her whole outlook brightened. She smiled. "Yeah! Yeah, you're right. I'm not going to quit. Thanks!"

"Wait, what?" Jimmy asked, totally confused. "You were going to quit?"

"I was thinking about this place like it was some scary, alien, grown-up planet," True explained. "But it's not. It's just high school."

"High school's pretty scary," Jimmy said.

"Naahhh. . ." True was feeling much more confident all

43

of a sudden. High school was familiar. She could handle high school. Now she knew exactly what to do. "Excuse me," she said, heading out of the office.

Jimmy called after her. "Hey, what's your name?"

True popped her head back in. "True. True Jackson," she said.

Chapter 5

Amanda and Cricket were still laughing by the elevators. The other woman was still there, too. True stopped to listen. They were still making fun of her. She would come up with a solution to the suit problem later. Right now she intended to set these grown-up mean girls straight.

"Okay, okay," Amanda said with a laugh. "She's used to doing homework, but I think she's a real home *jerk*."

Cricket and the other woman cracked up.

True walked right up to the little group. "What are you, seven?" she asked

Amanda was so shocked she spit out her coffee, getting it all over Cricket.

"Hey!" Cricket yelled.

"You know, there are these girls in my class," True told

them. "We call them The Pinks, and they think they're so awesome because they stick together and make everyone around them feel small." True stopped and let her words sink in for a moment.

The women were all silent. Now it was their turn to be embarrassed.

"Well, you know what?" True continued. "They're not so hot."

"Was there a point?" Amanda snapped.

"Yeah," True said with a confident smile. She looked from Cricket to Amanda to the woman she hadn't even met yet. "Neither are you." She turned her back on the three of them and walked toward her office.

Amanda gasped.

Cricket raced after True. All of a sudden, she was ready to be True's best friend. Just like The Pinks when they felt threatened. "We showed them, huh?" she asked. "Team Jackson in the house!" She raised her hand for a high five.

True simply looked at her.

"You do the, uh . . . put your . . ." Cricket dropped her hand, embarrassed.

"Cricket, you're probably really nice somewhere under all of that . . . you," True said. "But for right now, I need to be surrounded by friends." She took a deep breath. "You're fired."

Cricket gasped.

Oscar was once again at the ready with a tissue. Only this time the tears were Cricket's, not True's.

Amanda had heard the whole thing, too. She couldn't wait to let True know that she was making another huge mistake. "If you think you're going to make it without an assistant, then —"

"I'm not," True said, cutting her off. "I know the perfect assistant."

A little while later, True had laid out her whole plan for Lulu.

"No way. Forget it," Lulu said firmly.

"Come on, Lulu, free drinks in the fridge," True said.

Lulu crossed her arms over her chest. "*Nooo.*"

"All the clothes you could want," True said, trying to tempt her.

Lulu flipped through the mail on True's desk. "Sorry," she said.

True wracked her brain for something that would entice Lulu to work at Mad Style. She needed an assistant she could trust, and that was Lulu. Suddenly she had it! The thing that would convince Lulu to say yes. "Male models," she said.

Lulu's whole face lit up. "When do I start?" she asked.

True was about to say "five minutes ago" when Ryan rolled into the room on the back of a clothes rack. There was a sheet draped over it. "Check it out, ladies," he said happily. He pulled the sheet off, and there were the missing clothes! "Suits, y'all."

"Ryan!" True rushed over and ignored the stench of garbage to give him a big hug.

"You found them!" Lulu yelled.

True looked at the clothes. They didn't exactly look like they were ready for the Mad Style runway. "Oh, these are suits?" she asked.

"Yeah, there's some serious gunk on one of them, and this one's missing a teeny, little part of both entire sleeves, but it's good," Ryan said.

True flipped through the hangers. "I can fix that," she said, pointing to a tear. "And maybe I can cover the gunk. Lulu, go to the production department and see if you can find some fabric dye."

"You got it," Lulu said, setting off.

"But don't get distracted on the way," True said.

"Distracted? That's really insulting," Lulu said. But she forgot all about the insult when she spotted the blinds on True's office window. She hadn't noticed them before. "Cool shades!"

she said. She opened and closed the blinds, then opened and closed them again, and again, and again.

"Go!" True yelled.

"Okay!" Lulu said, rushing off.

True examined the suits again and then looked at the clock. If she was going to save this disaster, she had to get busy. There was way too much work to do, and not nearly enough time to do it in.

By her twelve o'clock deadline, True had done everything she could to bring the garbage-damaged suits up to Mad Style standards. She just hoped Mr. Madigan didn't look at them too closely.

The executives gathered in the conference room. True made sure the models were dressed and stood next to the runway. Lulu closed the curtains and dimmed the lights. True wanted as much drama as possible in the fashion show, plus the dim lights would hide some of the damage to the clothes.

When she had everyone's attention, True made the speech she had practiced in her office. "Mr. Madigan, assembled guests, it is my honor to present a variation on the wonderful designs presented yesterday by my esteemed colleague, Amanda," True said.

There was some applause around the room. Amanda seemed

surprised by True's compliment. She stood and made a small curtsey.

True turned to Lulu. "Music, please," she said.

Lulu hit play and some fun techno music filled the room. It captured the spirit of the new designs much better than the classical music Amanda had played the day before. The curtain rose and two female models paraded down the runway. They were wearing black business suits, but both had bright pink accents on their skirts. One had a big pink flower on her lapel; another wore a pink scarf around her wrist.

Ryan marched behind them. True hadn't been able to find the right male model on such short notice. Ryan strutted his stuff in a black suit with a hot pink tie. Then he got a little carried away. He unbuttoned his jacket and launched into a goofy dance. Lulu had to pull him off the runway!

True cleared her throat nervously while Lulu turned the music off. "Questions?" she asked, looking around the room. "Compliments?" she added with a hopeful expression.

Mr. Madigan walked over to one of the models and took a close look at the fabric she was wearing. "Interesting texture. What is that?" he asked.

"Garbage," True admitted.

"Bold choice," Mr. Madigan said nicely.

True couldn't let him believe she had done that on purpose. She babbled an explanation. "No, see, they accidentally got thrown out and we couldn't find them, but then we could, but they were sort of dirty, so I steamed them, covered the stains, and re-stitched the parts that got torn."

Amanda saw her chance to make sure True got fired. She jumped to her feet. "That is the most atrocious—"

Mr. Madigan cut her off. "Good thinking," he said to True.

Amanda finished her sentence without skipping a beat, taking her cue from her boss. "—but inspired resolution to a very difficult situation that I have ever heard." She smiled at True. "Nice job, moppet."

True smiled happily.

"I like the splashes of color. They're subtle, but distinctive," Mr. Madigan told True. He nodded to the room. "Approved. I'll see you all tomorrow," he said, quickly leaving the room.

True couldn't believe it. Just like that, her designs had been approved. In a few months they'd be in all the stores, and people would be wearing them to work. It was completely amazing.

Amanda rolled her eyes, but it was all True could do not to jump up and down with happiness. She walked over to Amanda and smiled. "I have a feeling we're going to be great friends," True said sweetly.

Amanda pretended to smile back at her for the benefit of the people around them. Then she growled as she left the room.

Lulu ran over and turned True around so that she was facing the door. Jimmy was leaning in the doorway with a huge smile on his face. He pointed his drumsticks at True and gave her a quick wink before moving on with his mail cart.

True and Lulu both squealed and then did their secret handshake. First, they slapped their palms together, then the back of their hands. Next, they clasped hands and pumped them up and down twice before snapping their fingers two times.

"Baby boo!" they said in unison.

After the meeting, True and Lulu headed back to her office. True had been so busy before that they hadn't had time to take in her new furniture — a super-comfortable couch with bright pillows, a cozy chair, and a mini-trampoline under a basketball hoop.

Ryan jumped on the trampoline and practiced his jump shot while True worked on a design sketch and Lulu handed True some fabric.

True stopped a moment to take it all in. She had become the youngest executive in the history of Mad Style! The job

was challenging, but True had stopped thinking that she was going to fail.

With her natural talents, the support of Mr. Madigan, hard work, and her good friends by her side, True could do anything!

Part 2

Firing
Lulu

Chapter 1

It was another busy day at the offices of Mad Style. People rushed on and off the elevators. Executives ran from one meeting to another. Garment racks full of the latest fashions were wheeled across the floor.

Oscar calmly fielded one phone call after the other at the reception desk, transferring callers to the correct offices. The phones got so busy that he had to ask some callers to wait. "Mad Style, please hold," he said. "Mad Style, please hold."

When he had a moment, he went back to them with, "Thank you for holding. How may I direct your call?"

On the other side of the office, Amanda's assistant was busy answering the phone, too. "Amanda Cantwell's office," she said. "She's in a meeting; can I have her return your call?"

In fact, all of the assistants at Mad Style were busy answering phones, managing schedules, and getting materials ready for design and production meetings. At least, all of the assistants except Lulu. She leaned back in her chair, plopped her pink-slippered feet on her desk, and chatted on her cell phone while she played with a cootie catcher. True's phone rang just as often as the other executives' telephone lines. The only difference was that hers went unanswered.

"Okay, pick a color," Lulu said into her cell. "Orange," she repeated. Then she spelled the word while she folded the cootie catcher one way and then the other. "O-R-A-N-G-E." She lifted the flap to reveal the fortune underneath. "Okay, you're going to marry for love *and* money!" she said happily, bouncing up and down in her seat.

True walked out of her office and stood in front of her best friend's desk. She had on her serious, vice president face. "Lulu, you got a second?" she asked.

"Sure," Lulu told her. "Hey, um, I've got to go," she said into the phone. She flipped her cell closed and turned back to True with a smile. "Ryan says hi. He's making a cake out of squeezy cheese."

True didn't care about cootie catchers and cakes at the moment. "I just got an IM from our factory saying they never got the designs for my accessories line," she said.

Lulu looked down at her cootie catcher and unfolded

the paper she had used to make it. There was a drawing of a cute blue-and-gray checked hat on the other side. "Oh, this one? It's so cute. I would totally wear this," Lulu said enthusiastically.

True snatched the paper away from Lulu. That was her design, and all the details were due at the factory yesterday if the accessories were going to be ready for Mr. Madigan's approval. She couldn't believe Lulu had turned her hard work into a fortune-telling toy. "Lulu!" she yelled.

"Hey, grabby, that's my cootie catcher!" Lulu yelled, yanking it back.

True was majorly stressed, and Lulu wasn't helping. This was her first big design presentation, and she wanted everything to be perfect. She took a deep breath and reminded herself that Lulu was more than an assistant. She was her best friend, too. She considered her words carefully. "Lulu, I love you, but I'm super-nervous about my presentation and I just need—"

True was interrupted by an annoying and ridiculously loud ringtone. Of course it was Lulu's cell phone.

"You know, I should probably get this, it could be important." Lulu flipped her phone open. "Hey, what up, Ryan?"

Amanda popped her head out of her office, delighted to hear that True was having some trouble. "So, you might not

58

be prepared for your accessories presentation?" she asked with tone of triumph in her voice. "I couldn't help but overhear."

True smiled to show Amanda that things weren't as bad as she hoped they were. "I know, I saw your ear pressed against the glass," she said.

Amanda tried to lie with a lame excuse, but it was pretty obvious she had been eavesdropping. "Yeah, well, I happen to do that to cool my ears," she said.

True knew that Amanda couldn't wait for her to fail. She pretended to be calm and in control. "Well, don't worry about my presentation," True assured her. "Team Jackson's got it all under control."

At that moment, Lulu let out a long, high-pitched scream. "Ryan saw a mouse," she said, when she realized True and Amanda were staring at her.

Amanda smirked at True. It was totally clear to her that True didn't have anything under control, especially her assistant. Team Jackson was going down and nothing would make Amanda happier.

All True could do was grit her teeth, smile for Amanda's benefit, and pretend nothing was wrong.

The next day, a number of Mad Style employees milled about in the conference room, getting ready for True's first big presentation. Amanda breezed in and started handing out index cards.

"One for you," she said. "And, this one is for you. There you go. . . ." she handed cards to two men in suits. Then she spotted True, who was getting ready to take a seat at the conference table.

"There you are, True," Amanda said, handing her an index card.

"What's this?" True asked suspiciously. She knew that Amanda had been trying to get rid of her since she arrived at Mad Style. No doubt this was another attempt to make her look bad.

"In my ongoing effort to increase productivity, I've come up with a system to speed up the pre-meeting process," Amada said importantly.

True looked at the card she was holding. She had thought Mad Style was a little too much like high school. Now she realized she might have overestimated things. "A seating chart? What is this, third grade?" she asked.

Amanda gave True a pointed look. "It feels that way sometimes, yes."

True took a closer look at the seating chart Amanda had given her and tried to find her chair. Her name was missing. "I don't see my name on this chart," she said.

Firing
Lulu

TRUE
JACKSON
Vice President

Amanda smiled. "That's weird," she lied. She turned to the rest of the room and clapped her hands for attention. "Everyone, please take your seats," she announced. "Oh, and if for some reason you don't have an assigned seat, please don't get in the way of those of us who do," she said, giving True another very pointed look.

No one wanted to face Amanda's wrath if they were too slow. True almost got run over when the other executives rushed to their seats.

Someone from accounting knocked into her.

"Sorry," True said, turning one way.

But then True was in the way of the people from the production department, scrambling to find their seats.

"Excuse me," she said, turning in the other direction. She backed up to avoid the crowd and fell over onto the runway that stretched between the two conference tables. Embarrassed, she hopped up as quickly as she could, but the whole room was staring at her. She could feel the red blush creeping into her cheeks, but she tried to pretend nothing had happened. "Some weather we're having, huh?" she asked.

Mr. Madigan rushed into the room and spotted True standing on the runway. All of the other executives were seated and

waiting for him to start the meeting, but True still stood in the middle of the room. She was simply looking for an empty seat, but to Mr. Madigan, it looked like she was taking charge.

"True, I thought leading the presentations was my job," he said.

Now True was really embarrassed. She started to babble. "No, um, you see there's this new seating chart and everything got kind of crazy, I just thought—"

Mr. Madigan cut her off. "Because, frankly, being the boss is a giant drag. So many times I come in here and everybody's just sitting here waiting for me," he said. "Thank you, True, for your thoughtfulness."

True smiled at him and then glanced at Amanda. She could see that Amanda was totally annoyed. Her plan had backfired. Not only did Mr. Madigan not mind that True looked like she was taking charge, he thanked her for it!

"It's all good. I mean, it is my accessories line after all," True said with a smile.

Mr. Madigan waved True on. "The floor is yours, milady."

True stepped up onto the runway again and got ready to show her colleagues just how good her accessory designs were. She might have been a little insecure about holding her own in a room full of executives, but True was totally confident about her designs. She knew teens and she knew fashion.

"Ladies and gentlemen, the life of today's teenager is busier than ever," she told the room. "There's school, homework, and after-school jobs. But that doesn't mean we have to sacrifice fashion. So, I give you my new line of accessories for the teen who's on the go!"

On True's cue, music began to play, and the curtain in the back of the room flew up. A few seconds later, one of Mad Style's teenage models strutted out on the runway. No one looked at her clothes, they looked at what she was carrying—True's design for a fun and fashionable umbrella.

When the model got to the end of the runway, she posed and opened the umbrella. It was a cool design, but there was just one problem—the umbrella was too small to keep anyone other than a baby doll dry. It was the world's smallest umbrella!

True was confused. She had designed that umbrella, but it was supposed to be normal-sized. Not this teeny thing. "What the—" she started to ask, but another model had already started to parade down the runway.

He was trying to strut to the music, but he was also trying to carry the world's largest backpack and it slowed him down. It was huge! Bigger than the model almost. It looked more like a tent than a backpack.

"See, that's a little bigger than I thought," True said nervously.

A third model made her way down the runway. This one was wearing the hat True had designed — the one on the back of Lulu's cootie catcher — but like the umbrella, it was super-small. It looked ridiculous on the model's normal-size head. It was a doll's hat, not a human's. Unfortunately, when the model got to the end of the runway, she pulled her arm out from behind her back to check her watch — another one of True's designs. Only, like the backpack, the watch was enormous. True cringed. *You could hang that thing from the tower at City Hall and it would be readable from all over the city,* she thought. What had happened to her cool wristwatch?

Amanda was whispering to Mr. Madigan.

The music stopped and the entire room simply stared at True. She herself was speechless. How had her great designs turned into such a huge disaster?

Mr. Madigan got up to examine True's work more closely. He peered at the hat. "Nice stitching, quality fabric. Alarmingly tiny," he said. "True, help me understand your vision."

"To be honest, I'm trying to understand my vision, too," True stammered. She didn't know what had happened to her designs.

64

She ran over the details in her mind trying to figure out what had gone wrong.

"You know what would help your vision with that hat? A magnifying glass," Amanda joked. She raised her arm up in the air. "Up high," she said to the guy next to her.

It was the same guy who Mr. Madigan had threatened to fire last week if True missed her deadline. Now he did what Amanda told him to do.

Amanda slapped him a high five.

"Kopelman! Don't be rude!" Max snapped at the man. "Out!"

"I don't know what happened," True said to her boss. "I mean, I did the drawings, selected the colors, and then I dictated the sizes to Lulu . . ."

Mr. Madigan's face registered Lulu's name.

Uh-oh, True thought. All of a sudden, she realized what had happened to her designs — Lulu had happened. She must have sent the wrong specifications to the factory. And she was too busy chatting on her cell phone and telling fortunes with her cootie catcher to notice.

True looked around and saw that everyone else in the room figured it out, too. Especially Mr. Madigan.

"By dictated, I mean I did everything on my own without

involving anyone else. Especially my best friend Lulu who had nothing to do with any of this," True said quickly. She didn't want Lulu to get into trouble, but it was too late. It was obvious that no one in the room bought her explanation. Lulu had messed up, and everyone knew it.

Chapter 2

Later that day, Amanda was still working on her seating chart. If True didn't have a seat at the table, she thought, it was only a matter of time before she was pushed out of Mad Style entirely.

"Oscar, I'd like to get my seating chart cards laminated," she said, walking over to the reception desk. "Do you know if we have a laminating machine anywhere in the—"

Oscar didn't have to hear the rest of the question. He reached under his desk, grabbed a laminating machine, and plopped it in front of Amanda.

"No, that's too small," Amanda told him.

Oscar plopped a larger laminating machine in front of Amanda, but she still wasn't happy.

"No, that's too big," she announced.

Oscar was starting to feel like Amanda was Goldilocks and he was one of three bears. He set another laminating machine in front of Amanda. This one was medium sized.

"Perfect," Amanda pronounced. "Oh, I'm also going to need a—"

Once again, Oscar didn't have to hear the end of the sentence. It seemed like he had ESP, but really he just knew everything about everyone at Mad Style and could anticipate his or her needs. He handed Amanda an extension cord.

"Okay then," she said, heading back to her office.

The elevator doors opened with a ding, and True's friend Ryan skateboarded off the elevator and over to reception desk. He set his laptop down. "Hey, Oscar. Check this out."

Ryan clicked a button and showed Oscar his latest video. Oscar watched Ryan whistle as he walked down the street. There was a banana peel in his path, but Ryan seemed to be too busy whistling and looking around to notice it. Suddenly, there was a loud crash and a girlish scream, and Ryan landed in a heap.

Ryan watched over Oscar's shoulder, laughing hysterically at his own accident. "That was me falling down in that video. Isn't it tight?" he asked.

Oscar shook his head. "No."

Ryan's forehead wrinkled in confusion. That wasn't the answer he was expecting. "Tight means good," he explained.

Oscar nodded. "Yes, I know."

If he knew, then why did he say no? Ryan wondered. That video was hilarious. "I'm going to be an Internet sensation," Ryan told Oscar. "I'm Ryan-the-other-falling-down-guy-dot-com."

Now it was Oscar's turn to be confused. "Why is it the *other* falling down guy?" Oscar asked.

"Well, there was one already. What do you think?" Ryan asked.

"I love it," Oscar told him.

"Really?"

Oscar shook his head. If Ryan really wanted to know the truth, then his original answer was the right one. "No," he said again.

"Why? What's wrong with it?" Ryan asked.

"You can see the banana peel, so you anticipated it," Oscar explained. "I like to feel surprised when I see someone fall."

At that moment, a guy from the accounting department walked by carrying a stack of papers. He stepped on Ryan's skateboard by accident, slid across the room, and fell into a garment rack. He hit the floor, his papers went flying, and the

clothes ended up in a heap. It was all a total surprise, both to him and to everyone else.

Oscar burst out laughing. "Now, that's a fall," he said.

Mr. Madigan walked across the reception area carrying a cup of frozen yogurt. He stopped at Lulu's desk. "Hi, Lulu. Is True in?"

Lulu tried to be super-professional. She knew things hadn't gone well in the meeting. "Whom may I say is asking?" she asked in a serious tone.

Mr. Madigan looked from side to side. Was Lulu really asking him that question? "It's me, Max," he said, pointing to himself.

Lulu folded her hands in front of her. "I'm going to need a last name, Max. Ms. Jackson's a very busy woman and she doesn't take —"

True popped her head out of her office. "Lulu! That's Mr. Madigan. My boss," she said. "Who you've met a thousand times."

Lulu nodded and turned to Max with a superior air. "Ms. Jackson will see you now," she said.

Mr. Madigan walked into True's office. True was right behind him.

"Two things, True," he said, once they were far enough

way from Lulu's desk not to be overheard. "One: I finally tried that Happy Berry YumYum downstairs," he said, holding up his yogurt cup. "Delicious. Two yums is not enough."

"I know, right?" True agreed. She was the one who told Mr. Madigan about the delicious frozen yogurt shop in the lobby. "I like the Tangerine Tickle. Makes my nose itch," she said, rubbing her nose.

Mr. Madigan nodded. "I've decided to treat myself to a cup a day."

"Good for you," True told him. "And, what was the other thing you wanted to tell me?" she asked.

"You have to fire Lulu," he said simply.

True jumped back and shot him a surprised look. "I what now?"

"Look, True, you have an amazing talent," Mr. Madigan said. "But unless you have a strong support staff, the world will never know. You can't do it all by yourself."

"But Lulu's trying," True said. "Sure, she may not be perfect—"

Unfortunately, Lulu chose that moment to prove to the entire office that she wasn't perfect. "Has anybody seen my stapler?" she shouted. Anyone looking could have told her that she somehow had gotten her stapler caught in her hair.

Mr. Madigan eyed True sympathetically, but his message was loud and clear. Lulu had to go.

"But she's my best friend," True said sadly.

"I know, but she may not be your best assistant," Mr. Madigan answered. He headed back to his own office. "Too bad there's no job called Assistafriend," he said over his shoulder. "Or Friendistant, or Secrefriendy." He was already out in the hall when he came up with one last fake job. "Worky-time fun pal?"

He breezed down the hall, leaving True alone with her problem—she had to fire her best friend.

Later that day, True was still trying to find a solution her problem. She didn't want to have to fire her best friend. Maybe if she could prove to Mr. Madigan that Lulu was doing a good job, both True and Lulu could keep working at Mad Style. Sending the wrong design specs to the factory had been a big mistake, but there must be other things that Lulu did well.

True hit the break room for a hot chocolate and was carrying it back to her desk when she spotted Oscar sitting at the reception desk. He was in the middle of all the action. If anyone could tell her what kind of job Lulu was doing, Oscar could.

"Hey, Oscar, can I ask you a question?" she asked

Oscar nodded.

"Lulu's doing a good job, right?"

"She's so nice," Oscar said, hoping that True wouldn't notice that he wasn't exactly answering her question.

True did notice. "I know; we've been friends since the first grade. But she's doing an okay job, right?" she prodded.

Oscar smiled uncomfortably. "I like her hair," he said.

"Right," True agreed. Lulu had great hair, long and straight and shiny, but what True wanted Oscar to tell her was that Lulu was doing a good enough job to stay on as her assistant. "But she's doing a—"

Oscar cut her off. He didn't want to come out and say that Lulu stank as an assistant, but she was horrible. "Please don't make me answer again," he begged.

True sighed and trudged over to her office. She couldn't believe it, but she was actually going to have to fire her best friend. Lulu wasn't at her desk, and she hadn't even told True that she was leaving.

True found Ryan lounging on the couch in her office. He was holding a video camera in front of his open mouth and making "*ahhhh*" sounds.

"Hey, Ryan. Where's Lulu?" True asked.

"Oh, out getting her yo-yo restrung. I'm covering for her,"

Ryan said. He opened his mouth again and made some bizarre noises for the camera.

"What are you doing?" True asked.

"I have another idea for a website," Ryan explained. "It's going to be called Ryan's-tonsils-dot-com. I'm predicting a hundred billion hits within the first month alone."

A hundred billion hits of Ryan's tonsils? True wondered. One look at that would be too much for True. "Why would people want to watch that?" she asked.

"Uh, because it's awesome?" Ryan said defensively. He moved the camera even closer to his mouth and made gargling sounds.

True's phone rang. It was clear that Ryan wasn't going to get up and answer it, so True walked over to her desk and picked up. "True Jackson speaking," she said.

Her other line started to ring, and True put her hand over the mouthpiece for a second. "Ryan, can you get my other line?" she asked.

Ryan shook his head and made another gurgling noise for his camera. "No can do. I'm crazy comfortable."

True rolled her eyes. "Can I call you right back?" she asked her first caller. "Okay, thank you, bye."

She pushed a button on the phone and took her other call. "True Jackson's office," she said. It was the plant manager

calling about her designs. "Oh, hi, Mr. Chuffa. You still haven't gotten the designs? I am so sorry," True said. Inside she was steaming. She had asked Lulu more than once to make sure that Mr. Chuffa got the correct designs, and Lulu had assured her she would take care of it right away. She obviously hadn't. True sighed. "Okay, I'll take care of it right now," she said, hanging up.

She looked at Ryan. "I have to fire Lulu."

That got Ryan up off the couch. "What? Why?" he asked.

"She's doing a terrible job," True said, pacing across the office. "She's totally irresponsible."

Ryan paced behind her. "C'mon, True, I think you're exaggerating."

True stopped and looked him right in the eye. "She left you to cover for her," True said simply.

Even Ryan had to admit, leaving him in charge was super-irresponsible. "Yeah, that's not good," he said. Still, he wasn't ready to agree that Lulu had to be fired. True could come up with another solution to the problem. "You've had to solve bigger problems than this. Was it easy helping me pass Spanish?"

"I had to tutor you every night for a month," True remembered. *"Muy difícil."*

Ryan had already forgotten everything she taught him.

He had passed his final test and that was enough. "Whatever that means," he said with a shrug. "And what about that time I forgot my multiplication tables. What did you tell me?"

"That it was just like riding a bike," she stopped her pacing for a moment. "And then I had to teach you how to ride a bike."

"Exactly," Ryan told her. "And that's just what you have to do with Lulu."

True's whole face brightened. Ryan might have forgotten his Spanish and his multiplication tables, but he knew what he was talking about! She didn't have to fire Lulu, she just had to teach her how to do her job. It couldn't be any harder than tutoring Ryan in Spanish or teaching him how to ride a bike. "You're right," she said. "Maybe we've just got to start over."

True walked toward Lulu's desk.

Ryan followed her out. "Great idea. By the way, what are you doing after work?" he asked. "I've completely forgotten how to ride a bike. I mean, I know I put my foot through the wheel, but I can't remember what to do next."

Chapter 3

A couple of hours later, True had a plan to save Lulu's job—and her own. First she made sure Mr. Chuffa got those designs—in the right sizes. Then she planned Operation: Train Lulu. She walked up to Lulu's desk, ready to put the plan into place. After all, she thought, Lulu had never been an assistant before. How could she do a good job if no one had ever shown her what an assistant was supposed to do?

"Okay, Lulu, I know we both got thrown into these jobs without a whole bunch of training, but we're going to fix that," True said. "Starting right now, we are going to turn you into the best assistant in the history of Mad Style."

Lulu gasped. "Better than Mabel O'Grady?" she asked, pointing to a black-and-white picture of a woman at an old-time switchboard.

Mabel O'Grady was Mad Style's first assistant way back in the 1950's, and the best one they ever had. The plaque underneath even said so.

True had to get Lulu to focus on her own job, not Mabel O'Grady's. "First, we'll work on phones. I'm going to call my office and you answer," she said.

"Easy breezy," Lulu said with a smile.

True took out her cell phone and dialed her office number. After a second, the phone on Lulu's desk stared to ring. Lulu picked it up and in her most professional voice said, "True Jackson's office."

But the phone didn't stop ringing.

"Hellooooo?" Lulu said, totally confused.

"You have to press the button," True told her.

Lulu pressed a button and answered the phone again. "True Jackson's office. *Hellooooo?"*

Her voice boomed throughout the office.

Lulu looked at True, even more confused now.

"That's the intercom button," True said patiently.

"Sorry," Lulu muttered. She was still on the intercom. Her apology reverberated over the loudspeakers. She pressed another button, and this time all the phones in the office started to ring at the same time. The noise was deafening.

"How did you do that?" True asked.

Lulu started to panic. "I don't know. I'm just pressing random buttons." She spotted one she hadn't noticed before. "I wonder what this one does." Lulu pressed the button and all the lights in the office went out. Lulu had caused a power failure.

True looked around in horror while her colleagues scrambled to figure out what had happened to the lights.

Lulu stifled a laugh and pressed another button on the phone. She had finally found the right one. "True Jackson's office," she said happily.

So the telephone lesson hadn't gone so well. True wasn't ready to give up. Her next step in Operation: Train Lulu was to explain the filing system. Maybe if Lulu got that down, True's designs would end up in the right hands instead of inside Lulu's cootie catchers.

She showed Lulu a pink folder. "Okay, this is an invoice from Diamond Textiles. Where would you file that?" she asked.

Lulu's face clouded with concentration, then she brightened. "Under 'D' for Diamond?" she asked.

True smiled and gave her a thumbs-up. "Awesome. You want to do the honors?"

"Absolutely," Lulu said, taking the file from her boss. She

dropped it into the proper spot in the filing cabinet and closed the drawer. Only she was a little too enthusiastic. Lulu slammed it so hard that everything on the wall behind the file cabinet came crashing down. The file was in the right spot, but everything else was in a state of chaos.

Lulu cracked up. All True could do was stare at the destruction with a frown. Still, Lulu was her best friend, and True wasn't ready to give up. With a sigh, she led Lulu to the copy machine for another lesson in how to be a good assistant. So far, Lulu and the copy machine hadn't exactly worked well together. The whole office had complained about Lulu's paper jams.

"All right, did you load the feeder?" True asked.

"Done," Lulu said with a nod.

"Did you set the contrast level?" True asked.

Lulu nodded again and smiled. "Done."

"Great. Then all you have to do is press the green button," True explained.

"Heck, I can do that with my eyes shut," Lulu said. She put one hand over her eyes and blindly stabbed at the copy machine's buttons.

Suddenly, papers started to fly out of the machine. And when all the paper was gone, the machine belched and started to smoke.

80

"That wasn't the green button," True moaned as the air around her filled with smoke. She didn't think things could get any worse, but then they did. The fire alarm went off.

True and Lulu both looked up at the ceiling at the same time. The sprinklers opened up and water began to pour down on them. The entire office got soaked.

After everyone calmed down and True unplugged the copy machine, she and Lulu sat in her office toweling off their hair. Ryan was still there, playing with his video camera.

"What a day," True said with a sigh.

"Yeah, that was the most fun I've had since we started working here," Lulu said, laughing.

Fun? True was about to ask Lulu what had been so much fun about making the sprinkler system rain on the entire office when Amanda came in, wrapped in a towel. She handed True an index card.

"What's this?" True asked.

"You ruined my suede coat. That's the bill," Amanda said.

True cringed, noticing the price. Then she noticed something else about the card. "Why's it laminated?" she asked.

"Oh, it's because I didn't have one of your tiny umbrellas to keep it dry," Amanda said with a mocking laugh. She turned on her very high heel and stormed out of True's office.

"She's mad," Ryan said, watching Amanda go.

Lulu stifled a laugh. "She's not the only one." She started to imitate the chaos in the office when the sprinklers went off. "People were all, 'These sprinklers are ruining my work! I have a deadline!' It was hilarious."

Lulu and Ryan both cracked up.

True couldn't believe that Lulu had actually enjoyed that! As far as she was concerned, it was a disaster. This was a business office, not a playground, and she was a vice president! If Lulu kept messing up, True's job would be on the line too.

"You're missing the point," she said to Lulu, walking over to her desk.

Ryan had enjoyed the chaos. He thought True was totally blowing things out of proportion. "Whoa, Miss Gloomasaurus," he said to True. "Since when are you on their side?"

"There are no sides. This is a place of business, not a game of kickball," she said.

That gave Ryan an idea. He turned to Lulu. "Hey, you wanna play kickball?"

Lulu jumped to her feet. She might stink at making copies, but she was an expert at games. "Yeah! That thing can be home plate." She grabbed a binder and threw it to the ground. Then she started to look for more bases, and a ball.

True grabbed the binder. "Lulu, that's Mr. Madigan's design

book!" She looked at it to make sure it hadn't been damaged, and noticed some of Lulu's handiwork. "And you put fairy stickers on it?"

"Yeah. And I made a flip-book." She grabbed the binder from True. "Watch the snowman dance."

Lulu tried to flip the pages, but True pulled the book away again. It was important, and Lulu had drawn snowmen all over it! "I can't believe you!" she yelled.

Lulu put her hands on her hips. She was getting pretty tired of being yelled at all the time. "What, are you mad at me again?" she asked with a sigh. "You know, ever since you took this job, you've changed."

True shot her friend an *Are you crazy?* look. Of course she had changed. She had a big job. She had responsibilities. She wanted to succeed, and she couldn't do that without the right support. Mr. Madigan was right. "Yeah, and you haven't," she said to Lulu. "I think hiring you was a mistake."

Lulu's jaw dropped. "Mistake? We're best friends," she said.

"Well, maybe there's a place for friends and a place for work," True said seriously.

"What are you trying to say, True?" Lulu demanded.

True thought about the question for a minute. She had tried, really tried, to make this work. But Lulu wasn't a good

assistant, and True didn't want to fail Mr. Madigan just because she wasn't tough enough to fire her. "Lulu, you're fired," she said sadly.

Lulu's face went from mad to sad in less than a second. True could tell her best friend was about to cry, but Lulu ran out of the office before she broke down.

True slumped against the side of her desk. She hated, hated, *hated* the fact that she had had to fire Lulu. But she didn't have any other choice, did she?

Ryan watched Lulu run out of the room. "Wow, that was heavy," he said. He got up and walked over to True, afraid he was about to get booted out, too. "But I can still hang out here, right, burrito?" he asked.

True rolled her eyes. What had he been doing while she was tutoring him in Spanish? "It's *amigo*," she snapped.

Chapter 4

True sat on the floor of her office alone, peeling Lulu's stickers off of Mr. Madigan's design book. She was still going over Lulu's comments in her mind, and she couldn't help but argue with them a little bit.

"'You've changed, True. You're no fun,'" she said imitating Lulu. "Yeah, setting off sprinklers in the office was real fun," True muttered to herself. She pictured the chaos all over again. The people running, trying to protect their work. Trying to stay dry. Then she couldn't help it, she started to laugh. If anyone else had set the sprinklers off she would have thought it was hilarious.

"It was a little fun," True admitted to herself. Ryan's comments still stung too. "But seriously, I'm not a Gloomasaurus. Not even close. I'm a Funasaurus Rex." To prove her point

she threw her head back and erupted into a giant, dinosaur *"Roooooaaaaar."*

True was in mid-roar when she noticed Amanda standing in her doorway, holding a laptop computer, and taking it all in.

"I'm sorry, am I interrupting a meeting with you and one of your imaginary friends?" Amanda asked with a sneer.

"No, I was just clearing my throat," True said. She pretended to cough. "Dusty in here."

Amanda got to the point of her visit. "Do you have any idea how late you're working?" she asked.

True thought about what she had to do before she could leave for the day. "Another hour or so. Why?" she asked.

"Just curious," Amanda said innocently. She started to head back to her own office.

True figured out the real reason for Amanda's question. Amanda had been competing with True ever since Mr. Madigan had hired her. "You're waiting for me to leave so it'll look like you're working harder than me, right?" True asked.

"No. I happen to have a lot of work to do, thank you very much," Amanda said haughtily.

But Amanda's laptop gave her away. True heard a ding and then a robotic, computer voice. "Amanda, would you like to play another game of solitaire?" the computer asked.

Amanda angrily clicked at a button to get her computer to be quiet and started to leave the room again.

True followed her to the door. She needed advice, and unfortunately, Amanda was the only one who would understand True's problem. "Can I ask you a question, Amanda?" she asked.

"Well, make it quick, I'm busy," Amanda insisted.

Once again, her computer proved her wrong. Its robotic voice announced, "Total games played today, four thousand, three hundred and ninety-two."

Amanda's eyes widened and she stabbed another button. "You were saying?" she asked, trying to pretend that nothing had happened.

"How do you do it?" True asked. "I mean, you're here all the time, where do you find time for your friends?"

Amanda shrugged. "It's not that hard," she said.

"Really?" True asked.

"I made a choice: work over friends," Amanda said simply.

True couldn't believe that. Was Amanda serious? Who could live without friends? "You mean, you have no friends?" she asked.

Amanda waved her arm around the office. "Well, who needs friends when you have a fabulous job?"

Amanda might have believed that she didn't need friends, but it was super-clear to True that she needed something. Otherwise, she wouldn't be on such friendly terms with her computer and its games.

Her computer called her again. "Amanda? Yoo-*hoooo*," it said.

Amanda slammed her laptop shut. "Listen, True. When you first started here, I thought you would never last. I didn't think you were capable of making the hard decisions," she said seriously. "But now look at you."

True straightened up with a smile. She never expected praise from Amanda!

"I never thought I'd say this, True," Amanda continued, "but you're a lot like me."

A lot like Amanda? True was absolutely horrified. Amanda was all work and no play. Amanda saw all of her co-workers as competitors. Amanda was best friends with her computer. True didn't want to be like Amanda, not even a little bit. She tried to wipe the idea from her mind the minute it entered, but she found herself daydreaming about what life would be like in thirty years if she truly was a lot like Amanda.

True saw the Mad Style conference room. People were milling about the way they always did before the start of a meeting. None of them looked very happy.

True heard herself calling out to her colleagues before she could see herself. "People, people. Let's get settled, shall we?" She rushed into the conference room and paused dramatically in the doorway. She looked just like a version of Amanda. She wore a power suit, high heels, and an expression that meant business. "Now, I know it's New Year's Eve and you all want to go hang out with your friends," Future True snapped. "But I have no friends, so we're going to spend the whole night here at work."

A few people groaned.

True click-clacked into the room in her high heels, just like Amanda. "Who groaned?" she demanded. "I thought I banned groaning." She stood in the middle of the room and snapped her fingers to make sure she had everyone's attention. "Now, let's start by working with my new seating chart." She handed out index cards with the kind of insults Amanda often leveled at her co-workers. "One for you, tubby. And you, four-eyes."

Future True heard Amanda's voice yelling from the hall. "Did somebody say seating chart?"

She turned around to see Amanda steer herself into the room in a wheelchair. True thought she might be about thirty years old in this daydream, but Amanda had aged at least twice that much. She looked like she was a hundred! And she was still trying to compete with True!

89

"Nice try, moppet," Amanda said.

Future True cocked a hip and rolled her eyes.

"News flash: No one makes seating charts at Mad Style except—" Old Amanda's head dropped onto her chest and she fell asleep in mid-sentence.

True shrugged and turned back to the employees in the conference room with a fake smile, ignoring Amanda's loud snores. "Well, now that interruption's behind us, let's move—"

She was interrupted again when Future Amanda's head popped up. "News flash!" she yelled, and then dropped off to sleep again.

True gave the wheelchair a kick and it rolled out of the room. "Go back to bed, dear," she said with fake sweetness. She strutted across the room again with her index cards. "Now, back to my new seating chart which is very—" This time True interrupted herself, or rather her nose did. She sniffed suspiciously. "Does anyone smell chocolate?"

The curtain at the end of the runway rose, and there was Mr. Madigan, eating a cup of yogurt. He wasn't the slim and trim Max Madigan True had come to know. This Future Max was enormously fat!

He waddled down the runway. "*Mmmm.* Even after thirty-two years of eating this yogurt every day, it's still delicious," he said. He waved his spoon around and some of his yogurt

plopped to the floor. "Whoops, spilled some on my shoe," he laughed. He looked down, but his feet were hidden from his view by his gigantic stomach. "I think I'm wearing shoes," he said. "True, shoe check, please."

One thing hadn't changed in thirty years. True still did everything Mr. Madigan instructed. "Right away, sir." She got on her hands and knees and checked her boss's feet. No shoes. Just socks, and they were yogurt-free. "Nope," she said.

"Thank you, True. I can always count on you," Mr. Madigan said happily. "Mainly because you have no friends, so you're always here."

"Well, who needs friends when you have a fabulous job?" True asked with a smile. She threw her arm out elegantly, just like Amanda always did.

The Future Mr. Madigan looked around with a quizzical expression. "Where have I heard that before?" he asked. Then he remembered. "Wait, I know, you always say that."

True laughed knowingly as if to say that yes, she had no friends, and she didn't care.

"Well, if nobody has anything else," Mr. Madigan said. "I suggest we wrap up this fantasy." He took another big spoonful of yogurt.

True shook herself to bring her horrible daydream to an

end. Amanda was still standing in front of her, looking like her everyday, young self. True looked down to check her outfit—she was wearing her own clothes and cute little flats. No clickety-clackity high heels in sight. But not everything was like it was just before Amanda's shocking and unwanted compliment. True had come to a very important decision. She didn't want to be like Amanda—not a lot, not a little, not at all.

"You know what? You're right," she told Amanda.

Amanda nodded. "Wouldn't be the first time," she said.

"Sometimes you do have to make a choice between work and friends," True said. She understood now that that was true.

"It's a pretty easy choice, if you ask me," Amanda said.

"Yeah. It is," True agreed. Only she realized that her choice would be different than Amanda's. Amanda chose work over friends. True would choose friends over work.

She walked passed Amanda and over to the reception desk. "Hey, Oscar, did you see Lulu leave?" she asked.

"Yes," Oscar said.

"How'd she look?"

"A little like . . ." Oscar made a pitiful, on the verge of tears face.

True frowned. "That's what I was afraid of," she said.

Oscar brightened. He liked doing impressions. "Now want to see my Mabel O'Grady?" He didn't wait for a yes. He twisted his face into an impression of the woman in the photograph.

True laughed, and then set off in search of her best friend.

Chapter 5

By Sunday, True still hadn't been able to find Lulu and apologize. Lulu wouldn't take her calls, and it seemed like everywhere True looked for her, Lulu had just left. She was definitely avoiding True. They had never gone this long without speaking since they met in first grade.

True searched all over. Finally she found herself in front of Mad Style's office building. She headed into the Happy Berry YumYum shop. It was one of Lulu's favorites.

True came in just as Mr. Madigan was leaving with a cup of yogurt.

"Mr. Madigan?" True said, surprised to see him there on a Sunday.

"Hey, True, fancy seeing you here," he said. "Are you having a nice weekend?"

True sighed. "Not really. I fired Lulu and now she's totally avoiding me. I was hoping to find her here, but I don't see her."

"Well, I'm sorry to hear that," Mr. Madigan said. He took a big bite of his yogurt. "I'm sure she'll—" He winced and stopped suddenly. He grabbed his temples and moaned.

"Mr. Madigan?" True asked.

"Brain freeze," he said, waiting for it to pass. "Okay, I'm back."

True remembered how enormously fat the future Mr. Madigan had been in her daydream. She took the yogurt cup from him. "You know, Mr. Madigan, maybe you should cut back on this daily yogurt thing," she said.

Mr. Madigan looked at her quizzically.

"I'm just saying. In thirty-two years, you'll be thanking me," True told him.

"Maybe you're right," Mr. Madigan said, seeing how serious she was. "See you tomorrow."

True set the yogurt down on a table and walked up to the counter. Fred was working—True had gotten to know him in the days since she had started working at Mad Style. So had Lulu.

"I've been expecting you," Fred said.

"You have?" True asked. *Why was he expecting her on a Sunday?* she wondered.

"Well, Lulu said you'd come looking for her," Fred said. "And, as usual, she was correct."

"Well, do you have any idea where she is? I've looked everywhere," True said.

"Her apartment?" Fred asked.

"Yup," True answered.

"The balloon store?"

"Yup," True said again.

Fred seemed to know all of Lulu's favorite places. "The whistle museum?" he asked.

True nodded. "Yup."

"Well, maybe you should try your office," Fred said finally.

Her office? That was the last place she expected to find her. "You think she's there?" True asked.

Fred nodded. "I'm sure of it," he said, handing True a piece of paper. "She left you this note."

True opened it. "'Dear True,'" she read. "'I'm in your office. Lulu.'" She looked up at Fred again. "Well, why didn't you just give me this in the first place?" she asked.

Fred shrugged. He sort of liked Lulu's favorite places. It was a fun list.

96

True ran across Mad Style's empty reception area. No one else was in the office on a Sunday. "Lulu?" she called. "Are you here?"

"In your office," Lulu yelled.

True ran in. "Lulu, I'm so sorr—" She stopped short when she saw her office. She was totally and completely amazed—too amazed to talk, even. Her office was filled with boxes. A few had already been opened, and they were chock full of the hats, umbrellas, backpacks, and watches True had designed. They all seemed to be in the perfect human sizes and in perfect condition.

Lulu stood in the middle of all the boxes holding a clipboard with a proud smile on her face. "Hey," she said.

"Oh my gosh," True said, as soon as she could get the words out. "How'd you get all this here on a Sunday?"

"Simple. I just called Jerry over at the warehouse and had him rush production. Then I called in a favor with Bruno to get him to expedite transpo," Lulu said. "Then I supervised our team as we off-trucked downstairs at the loading dock."

True was even more amazed now. Lulu sounded organized and in control, and she had managed to accomplish something True couldn't have done herself. In fact, True realized

she didn't even know what Lulu was talking about. Transpo? Off-truck? And where in the world was the loading dock?

"Wow, the part I understood sounded amazing," True told Lulu.

Lulu smiled. "Well, I couldn't have done it without my assistant."

"Your assistant?" True asked.

Ryan skateboarded into the office, then flipped the board to show True the bottom. He had added the Mad Style logo to his skateboard. "Ladies," he said.

"When I saw how much work was needed to get these accessories finished, I knew I couldn't do it alone," Lulu explained. "I had to ask someone I trusted to help."

"And when Oscar wasn't available, she called me," Ryan added with a laugh.

Lulu had done a lot of thinking after True fired her. "True, I know how much you needed me, and I'm so sorry I let you down," she said seriously. "If you give me another chance, I promise I'll be totally professional," she added.

True had done a lot of thinking of her own. "That's just it, Lulu. I don't want you to be *totally* professional," True told her. "I mean, we're just kids. I don't need an assistant as much as I need a best friend."

Lulu smiled. "I think I can juggle both of those jobs."

"So can I," True told her.

"Does that mean I'm un-fired?" Lulu asked.

True laughed and put her hand on Lulu's shoulder. "I hereby un-fire you."

"With a raise?" Lulu asked hopefully.

A raise? True laughed and shook her head. A raise was definitely pushing it. "No," she said firmly

"Deal," Lulu said.

The girls did their secret handshake to seal the deal. They had invented this a little while after they met and became best friends. It was still fun. They slapped their palms together, then the back of their hands before clasping their palms and shaking their hands up and down twice. Then they snapped their fingers. They finished with a big hug.

True let out a relieved sigh. She had Lulu back as her assistant, now she could think about other things. Like what Ryan was doing with his plans to become an Internet sensation. "So, Ryan. How's the website thing going?" she asked.

"Well, I don't have the exact figures, but it's approximately one hundred billion hits less than I was expecting," he admitted sheepishly.

"Wow, that's so weird," Lulu said sarcastically. "Who wouldn't want to see the inside of your throat?"

"Ah, no worries. I've decided to exploit another one of my talents in making a new Internet name for myself," Ryan said.

True thought about Ryan's talents and tried to figure out which one he was talking about. "Ryan-the-guy-who-can-eat-fifteen-pieces-of-French-toast-in-one-sitting-dot-com?" she asked.

"Ryan-the-itchy-butt-guy-dot-com?" Lulu asked, thinking of another.

Ryan scratched his butt. It was certainly itchy. But neither of those were the talents he intended to exploit. He had an even better one. "Nope. Say hello to Ryan-the-other-moonwalk-guy-dot-com." He started to moonwalk across the floor.

True was actually kind of impressed. Ryan's moonwalking wasn't half bad, but he had to go backwards, of course, and he didn't exactly have a lot of room. Ryan moonwalked right into True's couch and then into a stack of boxes. He flipped over backwards and sent a number of boxes flying, landing on his back in the middle of True's rug.

Ryan realized that move had actually exploited two of his talents—moonwalking and falling down! That would surely be a huge hit. "Please tell me one of you guys secretly video-taped that," he moaned from the floor.

True and Lulu both laughed as they ran to help him up.

*   *   *

Monday morning was the start of another busy week for Mad Style. Oscar was working the phones. "Mad Style, please hold," he said. "Thank you for holding. How may I direct your call?"

Across the floor, Amanda's assistant was just as busy, fielding phone calls and deciding who to put through to Amanda and who to put off until later. "Amanda Cantwell's office, one moment please."

True's phone was ringing, too. But Lulu wasn't at her desk and the phone just rang and rang.

Amanda stepped out of her office. "What is that incessant ringing?" she demanded.

Her assistant pointed to the phone on Lulu's desk.

Amanda was mad, and when she was mad she liked to take it out on someone. She glared at her assistant. "You're fired," she announced.

Then she barged across the floor and into True's office. She spotted True and Lulu sitting on the floor. A look of complete disgust crossed her face when she realized what they were doing. They were *playing*.

"Moppet, I thought we talked about this," Amanda barked, waving toward Lulu's desk. "It's like nothing has changed."

"That's not true, Amanda," True said with a smile. "A lot has changed." She held up a cootie catcher.

Lulu laughed. "Six," she said.

"One-two-three-four-five-six," True counted. She stopped and lifted a flap. "Looks like you're going to be an astronaut," True read.

Lulu gasped. "Cool! Will you design my spacesuit?"

"You know it, girl," True said. She turned to Amanda, who was still hovering in the doorway. "Amanda, you want to join us?" True asked.

Amanda frowned. "Me join you? For what?"

"I figure, you've already got the fabulous job," True told her. "Maybe you could use some friends?"

"Yeah, come on," Lulu said, waving her over. "Pick a color."

"Pass," Amanda said, stomping out of the office. She slammed the door behind her, but a moment later she was back. "Okay, green," she said, clacking across the room in her high heels.

True worked the cootie catcher. "G-R-E-E-N," she said and got ready to lift the flap.

True realized that it didn't matter what the answer was. What mattered was that she had a fabulous job *and* fabulous friends. And she didn't see any reason why she couldn't have both!

From True to You

Whether you're going to the movies with your girls or scoping the mall for cute boys, it's always important to have the perfect outfit for any occasion! A perfect outfit doesn't have to be what everyone else is wearing—it should be something that makes you feel cool and confident, and looks perfect on you! And, of course, any outfit that can take you from a casual baseball game to the hottest party of the year gets extra style points! True Jackson definitely knows how hectic and crazy every girl's life can be, so here are a few fashion tips straight from True to you:

Find your perfect pair of jeans!

A pair of great jeans is an absolute must for every girl's wardrobe! And that's because jeans can be casual or dressy.

For a fun and funky day look, pair blue jeans with sneakers and your favorite T-shirt. For a more glam night look, wear the same jeans with a cute pair of sandals or heels, a cool belt, and a sparkly tank top! Or try mixing things up and wear your fave jeans under a sundress or pair them with a cool vest for a rocker look. The options are endless. Jeans go with everything!

Fashion FYI —

Jeans come in all sizes, cuts, and colors. Sometimes it can be tough to pick the ones that are right for you. There are a few tricks to picking the right jeans. Dark wash jeans always look a little dressier and lighter wash jeans look more casual. So if you want to get a lot of wear out of your jeans, choose a dark wash. Next up is cut. There are so many different styles, but these are the most popular: flare, boot cut, and skinny.

Flare jeans are very wide from the knee down. Your grandmother might remember them as bell bottoms! These jeans are perfect for girls who have a wild style and wicked fashion sense. For a wilder look, wear flare jeans with your most colorful tank top and your favorite pair of sunglasses. For a sleek night look, wear your flares with a black tank top and a pair of shiny black flats or flashy high heels.

Boot cut is a classic style that opens slightly at the bottom so boots can fit under them, which means these are great for colder months when you need to wear boots or bulkier shoes!

For a natural day look, wear boot cut jeans with earth tones like green, brown, or yellow, and add leather bracelets for the perfect touch! For a Boho chic night look, slip on boot cut jeans, a peasant top, and, of course, your hottest pair of boots!

Skinny jeans are slim throughout the leg and really cling to curves! These jeans are faves with models and actresses everywhere, and they always make a statement. So if you're a girl who loves to look trendy and stylish, these jeans are your match made in denim heaven. Wear skinny jeans with a ruffled top and flats for a fashion-friendly day look. If you want to spice your outfit up at night, combine skinny jeans, a shiny pair of heels, and a jeweled clutch for the perfect party look! Skinny jeans also look fab tucked into tall boots and paired with a tank and cool leather (real or faux!) jacket!

Don't get discouraged if it takes you a while to find your perfect pair of jeans. Try on lots of different styles and colors until you find one that makes you feel fab! You might need a different style than your best friend, and that's OK. It's better to rock a style that fits you well and makes you feel comfortable and confident than to follow a trend that doesn't work for you.

When in doubt, accessorize!

Accessories are like the frosting on a delicious cupcake! They can really make an outfit come alive. Even the plainest

T-shirt and jeans can look high-fashion when paired with cute wedge sandals and a bold, statement necklace. And your pale pink party dress? Try pairing it with a thick black belt and black pumps for a little bit of rock-and-roll edge. Some of the best ways to accessorize are:

1) Hair accessories

If you want a relaxed look, you can't go wrong with a hat. For girls who are super-active, a sporty baseball cap is the way to go! Match a baseball cap with a fitted tee, boot leg jeans, and stylish sneakers for the perfect on-the-go look. Girls who like to spend time in the sun should pair a cute straw hat with your favorite bikini and a colorful beach wrap. You'll protect your skin and look super-stylish!

Headbands are also a fun addition to any outfit. There are many different styles, so it will be easy to find one that is perfect for you! For a retro look, choose a sequined headband and little black dress. For a more modern style, sweep your hair back with a plain, skinny headband, and tie it in a pony tail. Or choose one with a bow, or feathers, or even a big flower to really make a statement with your hair!

2) Necklaces, Earrings, and Bracelets, oh my!

If you want to dress up an outfit, jewelry is the perfect choice!

Necklaces

Necklaces are a fashion must! For a little sparkle in your day, pick a necklace that has a short chain and a pendant. With so many designs out there, it'll be easy to find one that matches your style. To spice up a dress or a blouse for an evening out, choose a longer necklace that will draw attention to your wardrobe ... and you! And to really spice up a plain outfit, a large statement necklace can be the focus of your look.

Earrings

Earrings come in a variety of shapes, sizes, and designs. For a soft touch to a casual wardrobe, put on a cute pair of studs. For a bold fashion statement, rock a pair of dangling feather earrings with a white dress. If you want to add some sparkle to a night out, wear a pair of long jeweled earrings that are sure to impress!

Bracelets

Bracelets are a great way to add personality to a wardrobe. Combine a worn-out pair of ripped jeans and chunky bangles for a fun and laid-back style. For a more Bohemian look, put together a white peasant top with beaded bracelets. If you want to pump up an outfit, shine on with gold and silver bangles!

3) Shoes

For a casual day look, try wearing either sneakers or sandals. For a funkier look, put on a pair of colorful sneakers with your favorite jeans and a plain white T-shirt. For a trendy school outfit, pair strappy brown sandals with a jean skirt.

At night, make your outfit pop with a pair of wedges. So many girls think that adding heels to an outfit is the only way to dress it up. But every girl also knows how dangerous a pair of heels can be! So if you're a chica who needs a break from those sky-high heels, try wedges. Wedges are easier to walk on. And they are just as stylish as high heels! Wedges come in many different heights—including size "extremely close to the ground"—one of True's personal favorites! Pair wedges with a sun dress and clutch for a fun and flirty look!

True's Ultimate, Most-Important-Ever, Can't-Be-Ignored, Seriously-Secret-of-the-Universe-Kind-of-Stuff, fashion tip:

Are you ready for it?

Fashion is all about who you are. It's about expressing your individuality and showing the world your personality. Fashion is not about looking like everyone else. So stand out! That's the one piece of fashion advice True always follows. I mean, how do you think she became V.P. of a fashion company?